Dreaming of Forests

AMY LAURENS

OTHER WORKS

SANCTUARY SERIES

Where Shadows Rise
Through Roads Between
When Worlds Collide
The Complete Sanctuary Series

KADITEOS SERIES

How Not To Acquire A Castle
How Not To Ring The Hero's Bell (2020)
How Not To Take Over The World (forthcoming)

SHORT STORY COLLECTIONS

Of Sea Foam and Blood
Darkness and Good

NON-FICTION

How To Write Dogs
How To Theme
How To Create Cultures
How To Create Life (2019)
The 32 Worst Mistakes People Make About Dogs

Find other works by the author at
http://www.amylaurens.com/books/

dreaming of Forests

AMY LAURENS

AUSTRALIA

Print ISBN: 978-1-925825-72-5
eBook ISBN: 9781393163077

www.inkprintpress.com

National Library of Australia Cataloguing-in-Publication Data
Laurens, Amy 1985—
Dreaming of Forests
80 p.   cm.
ISBN: 978-1-925825-72-5
Inkprint Press, Canberra, Australia
1. Young Adult Fiction—Fantasy—Contemporary 2. Young Adult Fiction—Sports & Recreation—Camping & Outdoor Activities 3. Young Adult Fiction—Action & Adventure— Survival Stories

Summary: Deena's friends are stolen away in the middle of the night by a mysterious forest. Can she set things right fast enough?

First Edition: July 2019

THERE WAS A FOREST. That was the simple fact of the matter: there was a forest now, and there hadn't been before. Deena let the tent flap drop closed in front of her, inhaled steadily, and tried again.

Nope, still forest. She bit her lip, debating: go out and explore, or hide in the tent?

In the end, exploration won for the simple, practical reason that nature, as it were, was calling. So she caterpillared her way out of her downy sleeping bag, pulled her hiking shorts on over the black, fleecy leggings she'd slept in, zipped up her polar fleece jumper, crammed her grandmother's knitted beanie over her brown hair, and pushed her way outside.

The other tent was gone. For a moment, that made her pulse race—but then the reality of her surroundings overtook her senses. The air inside the tent had been warm, musty. The air outside yesterday had smelled of the sea, a salty tang with just a hint of rotting seaweed.

Today, the air smelled like sap, and living things, a green smell she associated with her grandmother's garden thanks to that summer she'd spent there when she was twelve, when they'd spent hours of days of weeks pruning and twining and tending, returning to the house only for meals and sleep, hands crusty with black dirt her grandmother called gold, under-nails caked with the stuff, elbows and knees stained black—and green.

This, Deena thought, was what every green scratch-and-sniff thing should smell like. Forget your apple, forget your lime; *this* was green. She inhaled deeply, and despite the oddity of the situation, felt her eyes light up as her body relaxed, melting into the space while at the same time inflated, buoyed, full. Something about this wondrous, spontaneous forest was familiar—and right.

She had no idea what the trees were, but they were tall, straight as ship masts or indigenous spears, thick and thin, rough-barked but paler than stringy barks, a brownish-grey, and the tiny, emerald, coin-sized leaves looked soft as butter, soft as petals.

Deena had tried keeping plants in their third-floor apartment back home, but somehow she could never remember to water them enough, or else she watered them too much and they died, thin and pustulant. She cried, every time, as her mother shook her head and made Deena walk them down to the communal skip bins in the alleyway behind the complex.

Her grandmother had consoled her on the phone each time, had promised that one day she'd have plants aplenty, more than she knew what to do with.

But one day wasn't soon enough for Deena—which was why she'd taken up hiking, of course. If she couldn't have plants at home, by golly was she going to surround herself with them in her spare time. So a forest? Amazing.

The other tent, her friends, vanishing? Less so.

Nature was still calling.

And the current cover situation was a little thin for her liking; yesterday, there'd been a handy thicket of salt bushes and something vaguely acacia-like between the grass and the sand dunes. Today, it was just open forest all the way down to the sand behind and to her right, and all the way up to the mountains ahead and to the left.

On the other hand, there didn't seem to be anyone else around.

Sighing, she attended to her body's needs, butt cheeks momentarily icing over as a wind whipped down from the mountain, setting the trees rushling and shushling—but it seemed like a freak gust and nothing more, and soon enough she was clothed and warm again—and hungry.

A brief forage in the tent revealed a couple of muesli bars tucked into the pocket of her raincoat, and of course, there were the packet soups in her hiking pack, and she still had a couple of litres of water.

Nothing to heat it with, though; Rachel had had the Trangia in her pack, and some time in the night—as was pretty usual, these days—she'd snuck into the boys' tent, taking her pack with her for a pillow. Which meant that all of the above—Rachel, boys, tent, packs, and cooking stove—were now gone.

Deena sat heavily on the stump by the front of the tent and dropped her chin into her hands.

It wasn't that she'd never believed in magic before—she'd seen her grandmother's garden, after all, and although she'd stopped protesting to the contrary so people would stop protesting her sanity, she knew full well she'd seen creatures in her grandmother's garden when she'd been little that had no right existing on this mortal plane.

But on the other hand, until now, magic had been content to merely linger in the background, a blurred, bokehed backdrop to real life, something vaguely sensed, but never fully realised.

What, Deena wondered, had made the difference today? Why now suddenly jump arrestingly into the foreground?

Or, she wondered, gazing around as the trees whispered secretively, why *here*?

Hmm. That seemed like a crucial question.

The tent, she felt, was light enough. It would be a bit of a headache to get the whole thing into her pack with her camping mat—yesterday, Rachel had been carrying half the tent, but that clearly wasn't an option today, and neither was leaving the tent be-hind—but she should be able to manage. Because as she saw it, she could either sit here all day, hoping and wondering whether the others would come back—or she could go explore this magical, magical forest that even now was layering calm over her like blankets, like she belonged here, and *find out* what had happened to the others.

It took about thirty minutes, moving purpose-fully, to down a couple of muesli bars, swirl a packet of soup into one of the water bottles and gag it down, and pack up all the gear. It did fit in her pack—only just, and she'd had to let all the straps out, but it wasn't too heavy, just bulky.

And so, with the legs zipped onto her hiking shorts, turning them into pants once more, with her heavy boots on and her beanie still crammed over her hair and her hands deep in the pockets of her emerald-green polar fleece jumper, and her dark blue pack sticking up over her head and weighing down her hips, Deena set off through the trees that had miraculously appeared, heading back approximately the way they'd come in the evening before.

The Australian bush was always fairly quiet, so it was some time before Deena realised quite how unnaturally quiet the scene actually was; she was, without exaggeration, the only thing making any sound, if you discounted the still-audible hush of the ocean and the sporadic rustling of the trees when the breeze picked up. No birdsong, no rustling of small animals that she could detect... Nothing.

It didn't worry her as much as it might have, the bush being as aforementioned a relatively quiet place anyway, but it was certainly something to note.

Yesterday, they'd come in around the mountain from the south, joining a track at its feet that followed the coastline north to the little cleared area they'd used as a camp. The air had tasted of salt and smelled like teatree as they'd pushed their way onto the narrow dirt track amid the tussocky grass.

Today, there were no teatree thickets, and although Deena had her map and compass and was perfectly adept in using them both, she still felt uneasy striking off the path into the midst of the unknown, with nary a familiar landmark in sight.

That was, of course, except the mountain. She glanced up at it, with her back to the ocean as she stood somewhere around the point where they'd joined the track yesterday—she knew that because there was the rocky promontory behind her, a tiny stub sticking out into the water no more than ten or twenty metres, but clearly once a lot more impressive because of the small chain of rocky little islands that led out from it.

It was a beast of a mountain, steep and covered in boulders and drop-offs—a fact now largely obscured by the monotonous, tall, straight trees of the spontaneous forest, but a fact nonetheless.

Still. Deena couldn't help but think that if she could somehow get to the top of the mountain, she might be able to get a better handle on whatever was going on.

Certainly, it was a surer route than striking off the path at random. And at least if she was going *up*, she couldn't get lost, spontaneous forest aside.

The fact that something in the forest seemed to be directing her that way, that the chill wind earlier had seemed to come from up there, that had nothing to do with it, of course. All she was after was the view, so she could determine how far this new, strange forest stretched, and see what she could do about getting out of it to find her friends.

And so, up the mountain she went.

Her underarms grew warm first, then the band around her hips and waist where the pack was buckled on. Her hands were the next to feel the effects of her exertion, growing puffy and hot.

She stopped once to shove her beanie into the pocket of the pack up above her head, and then a second time to take off the polar fleece jumper, wrinkling her nose as she caught a whiff of her own body odour as the jumper went over her head.

She crammed it into the top of the pack before drawing the pack's neck tight again, rebuckling it closed, and saddling up to continue on her way after a quick slurp from the lighter of the two water bottles.

The erratic wind breathed over her face, cooling her sweat, and it was pleasant for a fraction of a second as she lifted her chin to it, thumbs tucked under the straps of her pack—until she recognised the scent it carried as the late stages of decay. For the first time since the forest had appeared and her friends had *dis*appeared, adrenaline flashed through the pit of Deena's stomach.

She could go back down the mountain. Try to find her way back around, head back across the bush—forest—where they'd come, get to phone range, call for help. There might be service on top of the mountain, though. There sometimes was, if the mountain was high enough and clear enough, even out in the middle of nowhere.

The wind came again, down from the top of the mountain, and this time it spat raindrops in her face.

Absently, Deena thumbed them from her cheekbone—and startled as her thumb came away red.

A hurried investigation revealed that it had not been raindrops at all, but thinned blood—she'd sniffed it, trying to determine, and when that hadn't proved helpful, heart hammering, eyes scrunched closed as she wondered if this would be the first and last most stupid thing she'd ever do, Deena risked a quick taste, and the iron-y, metallic, slightly sweet sensation had been unmistakeable—except it was only bloody where it had landed on her; none of the surrounding vegetation had been tinted red.

It would take two full days to reach phone service if she went back the way she'd come.

Her pulse kicked.

Two days was a long time for her friends to be missing in the bush at this time of year. They had all the right equipment of course… Well, assuming they were still *with* the tent, and the packs, wherever they might be.

Of course, they might already—she swallowed hard and worked her tongue, trying to get the taste of blood from her mouth, wiping her hands compulsively up and down her thighs, palms, backs, palms, backs, up and down, up and down, up and down— they might already be dead. And if she went after them, she might be too.

But that was the catch in these sorts of situations, wasn't it? And they didn't exactly come with a manual to tell you what the right thing to do was.

You never split up in the bush, sure, but no manual covered what to do if all your friends and their belongings just spontaneously disappeared. Deena stared through the forest to where she imagined the crown of the mountain might be (it was almost impossible to tell how high it went through these trees), and bit her lip.

Suddenly, as though they'd been saying it all along but her brain had only just now tuned in to their language, the rustling of the trees in the breeze was her name, Deena, over and over and over again.

That set the adrenalin off again—but they were trees, and she loved trees, and anyway the way they were saying her name didn't exactly sound *ominous*. And if she let herself drop her guard for a moment, there was that sense of calm again, layering over her fears like warm, heavy blankets in winter, comforting and enlivening all at once.

Cautiously, Deena reached out to the nearest tree and pressed her whole hand against it. The bark was rough under her skin, and Deena worked her fingertips against it a little, feeling the cracks and crevices. The bark was slightly cooler than the surrounding air—which made the tree pretty cold indeed, because despite the heat from her present exertion, now that Deena had stopped she was cooling off fast, and the air couldn't have been much more than about twelve degrees.

(The predicted overnight lows for the hike had been in the high single digits, only a few degrees above freezing, and her mother very nearly hadn't let her come because of that, all the correct—and fancy—hiking gear aside.)

But anyway, the tree hadn't done anything to hurt her, and it, along with the rest of the forest, was whispering her name, and it was two days' hike to phone service, and she couldn't do anything for her friends if they were dead—of exposure or something, obviously, not anything magical, that would be ridiculous, and unnecessarily grim.

Deena shifted the pack, hefting it up higher on her hips, pulling the straps forward from her shoulders and tucking her thumbs under them again. Right. It was decided then.

And so, one step after another, with the shuffffff-clomp, shufffff-clomp of her hiking pants and hiking boots, Deena resumed her climb up the mountain.

The cloud cover was thickening, a silver lining over the whole sky, scudding by as the wind picked up, though the wind seemed to be coming predominantly from offshore now, which she would have expected around here, and that comforted her, the humid, salty wind dimming the intensity of the green smell around her.

Once, Deena thought she'd reached the top, cresting over a rise with her heart in her throat—was that the lingering taste of blood she could detect?—but it was only the peak of a spur, and in front of her was a hollow where the leaves of the trees turned golden, so they looked like shiny, brand-new dollar coins fluttering in the salty wind, flashing bright against the silver sky.

They were thinner than coins, though, leaf-thin, and they looked so fragile. Thin and—Ow! Deena sucked at the crescent of blood traced on her forefinger—razor sharp. What was the point of such leaves? she wondered. Still, they were pretty, and absently she pulled a twig of them from the nearest tree and twirled it in front of her as she walked.

Shuffff-clomp. Shuffff-clomp.

She tilted her head. A sound, something different.

Deena inhaled deeply, but it was wishful thinking to imagine she might smell anything but salt and sap right now. Still, the background sounds had shifted in quality a little, almost like—ah ha.

There, at the back of the golden-treed hollow, was a little bubbling waterfall, only a foot or so high, feeding a pond the size of Deena's two-person tent. The pond didn't seem to go anywhere, didn't seem to have an outlet—and when Deena leaned over it cautiously, the water was pitch black, bottomless.

She shivered, and tucked the little sprig of leaves into her front pocket, consumed by a sudden urge to have both her hands free, just in case.

Probably, there was an underground crevice or something where the water drained away. That was a perfectly normal thing that happened, right? The pond wasn't bottomless, it was just deep, and the lighting was hardly great what with the cloud cover and the tree canopy, so of course it looked black.

The fact that there were no reflections on its surface, apart from the occasional flash and snap of brightest gold, like one of the leaves was swirling over the little ripples, shimmering like—ha ha— gold leaf... Well, it was probably just the angle she was on.

The real question here was, did she dare fill up her water bottle. The one from this morning's soup was ready now—she'd filled it up from the creek near the clearing before she'd set out, far enough back from the ocean so it wasn't brackish, and had dropped in the purifying tablet to work its magic for half an hour—but the other one was down to the last cup or so of water.

There was no guarantee she'd come across water again while she was up on the mountain.

It was the safe, sensible thing to do.

And running water was cleaner, everyone knew that, and that's why she climbed up a few metres above the pond, above the waterfall, before taking the lid off her bottle and plunging it into the sharp, icy water—common sense, and nothing at all to do with the uneasy, unearthly feeling she got standing near that pond.

The stream led up the mountain. Well, the stream led *down* the mountain, because that's what streams did, but Deena followed it up the mountain like a path, keeping it a few metres away on her left as she climbed through the same tall, straight trees with their greyish, rough bark and round, coin-like leaves that, now she was out of the hollow, were bright green once again.

She could have sworn the mountain was less high than this. Oh, for sure, you always ended up underestimating how long it would take you to climb any given mountainside, but even bearing that in mind, Deena was sure she ought to have reached the top by now. And yet, shielding her eyes with her hand and peering through the silvered light, she could no more spot the top of the mountain through the trees than fly there.

So she kept walking. And walking. And walking.

Every so often she'd have to stop, dropping her pack to the ground and wriggling out of it, circling her shoulders to release the slow-growing burn in them. She'd retrieve a water bottle from one of the pack's outer pockets and sip slowly at the ice-cold, slightly chlorinated water as she sat on the lumpy mass of her pack and stared back the way she'd come.

The forest was open, and she could see downhill a fair way, even spot the occasional glimpse of ocean through the trees—and it seemed very, very far away.

Deena chewed the inside of her lower lip as she gripped the plastic water bottle, cold against the tips of her fingers. Surely the mountain hadn't been this high before.

A quick check of her phone revealed that she was still out of service range, so she turned it back off to preserve the battery and tucked it away, took a last sip of the chemical-ly water, recapped the bottle, and tucked it into its pocket as well.

She stood, stretching out her lower back, then stooped, grabbing one shoulder strap of her pack that was beginning to smell distinctly sweaty.

A movement downhill through the grey-brown trees caught her eye.

Deena straightened without the pack, and stared.

It took nearly a full minute, but at last she spotted something, grey-brown like the narrow tree trunks, sitting on its hind legs fifty or so metres down the slope and watching her with pricked ears. It looked almost like a kangaroo, a big silver-brown one, probably a male given the buffness of its chest and forearms, only…

Deena swallowed and broke eye contact, turning and gathering up her pack, hefting it into place as though the weight of the pack was the reason her heart was hammering, and not the look in the almost-kangaroo's eye.

Deena set out again, a little faster this time than she had been, shuufff-clomp, shuufff-clomp, shuufff-clomp.

Crackled footsteps, slow-moving, behind her.

Deena whirled, pack spinning her around with its weight.

The not-quite-kangaroo stared at her from a scant twenty metres.

Crackling in the leaf litter to her right.

Another not-kangaroo, staring at her in the same blood-chilling manner, as though they recognised her perhaps—or like today was the day they had decided to give up on vegetarianism and see what the whole meat-eating thing was about.

Deena's teeth clenched. She whirled back uphill and went a little faster again.

A third kangaroo meandered on all fours out of the trees on her other side, gaining far more ground with every gentle, slow hippity-hippity than it should have.

Her heart was pounding at her chest, and as it did, the ground in front of her grew steeper.

It hadn't been that steep a moment ago. Deena blinked, breaths coming in short gasps, fingers knotted around the straps of her pack, pulse racing.

Behind her, on both sides, the disconcerting stare of the kangaroos drew closer.

In front of her, the land seemed to tip, until the way was slippery with damp, half-rotted leaf litter, the smell of it winding about her as she slipped and stepped and slipped some more, flinging her hands out and down to the ground for balance.

The kangaroo on her left coughed.

Deena squeaked, scrabbling at the ground that was rising, rising.

In a second, it would be nearly vertical, and she'd go sliding back into the kangaroo behind her, with his bulging muscles and wicked-sharp claws and that glint in his eye...

Deena gasped. Up, she had to get up.

She flung out a hand to grab at the nearest branch, trying to haul herself up the slope, up and away.

There was a kangaroo in front of her, blocking the way as it loomed over her, sitting upright and at least a couple of metres tall.

Deena stared, wide-eyed, frozen—and the roo held up one front paw, claws outstretched, then slashed at her, fast as lightning.

Deena screamed as the claws sliced through the sleeve of her shirt, tearing ribbons in her skin. Fire burned in her arm. She crouched, hunching to protect herself with her pack, gripping her shredded, dripping bicep tight as her pulse pounded and she braced for the next slash of claws.

Instead, a deep, echoing voice boomed out. "Ah, a sacrifice of blood. You greet me kindly, little one."

Heart still pounding, the smell of blood thick around her and her arm stinging fit to burn, Deena tried to raise her head. But the pack was bulky, unwieldy, and her balance as she crouched precarious: the pack tipped, and she went with it, sprawling ungainly on the ground. Adrenalin spiked through her as she waited for the weight of the pack to drag her down the hill—but she lay still.

Abruptly, she realised that it wasn't dark because she had her eyes closed, and that the surface she was lying on was neither leaf litter, nor sloped.

Another round of adrenalin kicked through her body.

"You should find it much easier to move without your burden," the deep voice said, amused.

Deena lay still, her heart pounding, blood pulsing through her stinging, shredded arm, her back aching as she lay awkwardly over her pack. Around her, everything was dark. She couldn't see her own body, couldn't see the owner of the voice—or the trees, or the kangaroos... Her heart jolted. The kangaroos. The voice had mentioned a sacrifice of blood.

She shuddered without meaning to.

"Come now," the deep voice said, and tutted its tongue—assuming it had a tongue.

It was speaking; it had to have a tongue. Right?

But a tongue meant a mouth which probably meant teeth and it had said sacrifice, a blood sacrifice, and the darkness abruptly felt too hot, smothering, and Deena couldn't breathe, and she was gasping, gasping...

Some tiny, rational part of her knew that she was hyperventilating, but, as ever in such situations, the knowledge did little to help her.

Nothing, in fact, did—until something suddenly released the pressure of her pack's straps with a sawing noise, the sound of snapping fabric; and something with cold, hard, pointy-tipped fingers helped her sit up.

"There," the deep voice said, and now it was coming from right beside her. "Deep breaths now. Deep breaths."

Deep breathing would be a lot *easier*, she thought, rolling her eyes side to side in the darkness, if she hadn't abruptly realised that the *thing* didn't have fingers at all; those had been claws helping her upright, long and incredibly strong.

But still, she obeyed, sucking air in very slowly through her nostrils, the smell of blood no longer so strong, and forcing it out through pursed lips.

"There," said whatever it was. "That's better now, isn't it."

Deena wasn't sure. Obviously she wasn't hyperventilating anymore, and that was a good thing, but on the other hand the darkness still felt heavy and close, she still couldn't see a thing, she'd cut the inside of her mouth and if she couldn't smell blood now she could definitely taste it, and if truth be told, she suspected she wasn't entirely on Earth anymore.

Which was absurd.

But so was a spontaneous forest, and trees with razor-sharp leaves, and a pool that looked like a portal, and the kangaroos, and whatever this *thing* was in the dark here with her.

On the other-other hand, she realised, her arm didn't hurt any more. Hesitantly, she touched it, running cautious fingers over her bicep. Flaps and ragged bits of shirt, drying blood… But no wound. She bit her lip.

"Oh," said the voice, "do pardon me. I always forget how terrible your night vision is."

Abruptly, a light switched on. Deena scrunched her eyes closed against the sudden flood of brightness, flinging up an arm to shield them.

"Oh, is that worse?" the deep voice inquired with a note of concern.

Deena slitted her eyes open under cover of her arm and managed a hoarse, "No."

She squeezed her eyes, blinked a few times, squeezed some more, and eventually, when it no longer felt like they were going to be burned out of their sockets by the sudden influx of light, Deena lowered her arm and opened her eyes properly.

They promptly widened as far as they could at the sight of the creature peering down at her with furrowed eyebrows—eye ridges—eye… parts.

For the creature didn't have hair at all, and neither did it seem to have skin.

In fact, it seemed as though it had something like moss-covered scales, and the tufts at the end of its vaguely horsey ears and under its sort-of-goatish chin were thick and strandy, like some of the thready lichen Deena had seen on previous hikes. It was the same colour, too: a pale, almost washed-out green, while the rest of the creature—the dragon, obviously, because plausibility aside, it was very clear that she was being carefully inspected by a mossy, planty kind of dragon—was a range of darker greens, from mossy brown on its face to a deep, emerald grass green over its body.

Its eyes, however, were a brilliant, rippling shade of metallic gold.

"Your breathing is quite fast," the dragon-creature said, frowning. "I wonder, have you lost too much blood?"

The question was, apparently, rhetorical, for the dragon leaned over and began prodding at Deena's arm with long, brown, and as Deena had previously ascertained, strong claws.

"Mmphrggg," Deena managed, still wide-eyed.

It's not going to eat me, she told herself sternly, forcing herself to sit still while it inspected her upper arm. *It's concerned for my wellbeing, and it's not going to eat me.*

Comments about blood sacrifices aside.

The dragon rocked back, tapping its chin thoughtfully. "No, no, the wound has healed quite nicely. I doubt you'll even have a scar, which is lucky, those kangaroo beasts do have quite the knack for tearing things up, nasty creatures. I've fairly sure they're just being vindictive, but I'll have another word with them again, there's no reason to hold onto the past, really. I'd have thought they'd have quite forgotten it by now, but you know marsupials. Longest memories there are." The dragon shook its head, tutting disapprovingly.

Deena finally remembered how to blink, then risked sucking in a long, rather desperate breath of air.

Something in her shoulder was catching, a muscle pulling funny. She shrugged her shoulder, rotated it around, and felt something pop satisfyingly.

She took a deep breath and blew it out through her mouth.

"There now," said the dragon. "Much better. Now. What did you have to ask me?"

"I... I'm sorry?" Deena said. She hadn't been intending to ask the dragon anything, of course—except perhaps who it was, and why it had suddenly appeared.

The corner of the dragon's mouth twitched, something that might have been meant as a smile. "Only those on a desperate quest can stumble so into my domain," it said with a hint of self-deprecating irony. "You must have been searching hard for *something,*" it continued in its normal tone. "It's the only way anyone ever finds me."

"My... my friends," Deena managed, suddenly struck with a sense of familiarity. Unless she'd suffered an amazing bout of amnesia at some previous point in her life, she knew she'd never met a dragon like this before. And yet, now that she'd acknowledged it, she couldn't shake the sense that she *knew* this dragon, or at least others like it.

"Ah, your friends." The dragon nodded sagely. "And why, pray tell, are you seeking them? Are they lost, or are you?"

"I... I'm not sure," Deena said, and bit her lip. "You see, we were camping—we've been hiking," she clarified as the story spilled out in a rush, tears tugging at her eyes. "And we were sleeping, it was nighttime, and Rachel had slipped out in the night to sleep in the boys' tent, and then when I woke up in the morning none of them were there, and the other tent was gone and so were they, and instead, there was just this… forest.”

Abruptly, she buried her face in her hands, shifting her hands downward almost at once and pressing all her fingers firmly against her eyes.

Crying didn't help anything.

“Ah,” said the dragon. “I see. I thought something like that might have happened. It explains the kangaroos, anyway. They have a sixth sense for things like this.”

Deena shook her head, fingers still pressing against her eyes. “Like what?” It came out a little more exasperated than she'd intended, but then, it was asking just a little too much of her to expect her to be rigorously polite right now.

“The forest,” the dragon said simply. “A spontaneous forest, appearing in the middle of the night, apparently at random, disappearing up all the people bar one.” It tilted its head at her, eyes gleaming.

But of course, Deena had no idea what it was alluding to. “Does that mean you know where the forest came from?” she ventured, not quite brave enough to add, ‘And how to get rid of it?’

The dragon sighed, and shrugged its mossy shoulders like a boulder shifting in a stream. “You called it, of course. While you slept. In your slumber, you dreamed, and in your dream you sang, and you called a whole forest into being.”

Deena blinked. That... was a little too much to process right now, quite frankly. "What about you?" she said instead.

"Me?" The dragon raised its tufty eyeridges, catching her meaning immediately. "Child. No. You could hardly dream *me* into existence; I am far, far older than you, for a start, and have been watching over you for many a year."

Deena shivered as the hint of familiarity gave way to the certainty of knowing. Eyes, tiny golden eyes like glass beads, in the dark dimness of her grandmother's garden, winged green lizards no bigger than her finger fluttering and flitting from branch to branch, blending and camouflaging with the greenery. The one tiny creature who'd seemed to have broken a hind limb—Deena had doctored it as best as a seven-year-old with limited medical supplies could.

This dragon was no different—just several orders of magnitude larger.

"You see," the dragon said, nodding once with satisfaction. "You know my kin. And so, if you want this forest to end, if you wish to be reunited with your friends, thus mote it be so; it is but a simple matter, for you called the forest into being, and you can very easily wish it back away. I shan't send you out the way you came in, blood sacrifices are rarely comfortable for anyone involved. No. Here you go, we'll do this the nice way instead." It turned away from Deena a little and raised its hands out in front of it, palms—such as they were—facing the ground.

Things were moving far too fast.

Golden trees and probably sentient kangaroos, magical darkness and kind-hearted dragons, and now the news that she, Deena, the most ordinary girl who had ever lived (except perhaps for her strange love of plants), had dreamt an entire forest into being—and that she could apparently wipe it away just as easily.

Only she had no idea…

The tune the dragon began humming as it moved its hands in slow, deliberate circles wiped conscious thought from Deena's mind and sent shivers down her back; somehow the dragon managed to sound like a pan flute and a set of chimes all at once, and the result was both startling and clearly other-worldly.

The result was, too: a shimmer of light appeared on the dark ground next to Deena—what *was* she sitting on?

No, best not to think of that, concentrate on the light—and it rapidly resolved into a little pond, only a pace across and deep as the world, jet black like the one Deena had seen in the golden grove, with the same shimmering flickers of gold in its depths, as though perhaps the spirits of goldfish swam therein.

"Right, in you go," the dragon said cheerily, stepping back and gesturing.

"What, now?" Deena said as clarity of thought came rushing back, now that the humming had stopped.

"No time like the present," it chirped. "Of course, my present isn't your present isn't the worldly present, but no matter. Off you trot."

Deena swallowed, but there was really nothing else for it.

She glanced back at her pack, its ruined straps flopping useless at its sides.

"Oh, no, dear, never mind about that," the dragon said, taking her by the shoulders and steering her at the pond. "That's a trifling matter. It will all be fine once you undo the forest. In you go now!"

Deena squeaked as the dragon pushed her firmly, though not unkindly, into the water, the icy cold shocking over her as she flailed to orient herself.

But surely she had to go *down*, since she was trying to get somewhere else? Up, down, up, down—it didn't matter anymore, because Deena had no idea which one was which in the pitch darkness of the water, and even letting herself go and float for a second didn't do anything to clarify the matter—what had *happened* to gravity?—and the pressure was starting to build in her sinuses, her face, as the deepest part of her brain instructed her body over and over again to breathe, to inhale, to find oxygen…

Something warmish broke over her face, and it took Deena a moment to sort through the sensations—her burning lungs, the intense pressure over her face, the ache in her hands and feet as the chill of the water set in—to realise that the mild warmth was actually the air.

She inhaled greedily, coughing and spluttering as a little of the water made its way in, flailing as she reached, eyes water-blind, for something to grab.

Her hands scraped against rock and she snatched at them, hauling herself to the edge of the pool, her body knocking against the vertical sides.

For a moment, she huddled against the rocks gasping, waiting for the fire in her lungs to still, appreciating the feel of air rushing deep into her chest, the solidity of the granite-like stones under her palms and fingertips, the smell of leaf litter and salt water humidity.

Gradually, she realised both that her body was functional once again, and that there was something odd about the smell of the place.

Deena hauled herself up out of the pond, kicking and flailing like a whale attempting to beach itself as she fought for purchase on the smooth, vertical pond walls—damn but she needed to work on her upper body strength—until at last she panted and gasped her way to dry land.

She lay there for a long, indeterminable moment, just enjoying the stability of knowing exactly what it was she was lying on, and then she blinked her way back to full awareness, eyes thick and a little crusty like it was first thing in the morning, tongue dry and sticking to the roof of her mouth.

Her tongue wasn't the only thing that was dry, she realised as she sat up.

A moment ago, when she'd been in-and-out of the water, she'd been soaked through, her hair plastered to her face, her shirt plastered to her body.

Now, although she could taste the lingering remains of the spring water in the back of her throat, she was perfectly, completely dry.

And she realised what was up with the smells, too: not that anything *here* was wrong, but that back *there*, there had been no smells.

That… made her all kinds of suspicious, actually, because she'd been in the water but was actually quite dry, and she'd had her arm torn up but both it—and now her sleeve—were actually quite fine, and although her dreams were often hyper-coloured and vivid, she couldn't remember once smelling anything in any of them.

Deena squinted at the scenery, letting the smell of foresty leaf decay and salt from the ocean drift over her, even though she wasn't breathing very deeply.

Still.

Her pack was definitely missing, which meant if she *had* merely dreamed the dragon, goodness knew what she'd been doing while she was.

A rustle in the leaf litter caught her attention, over and away to her left.

A great, grey kangaroo—the big, buff male from earlier, unless there was more than one hanging around—sat back on its hind legs and watched her with its piercing stare.

Deena got hurriedly to her feet and began moving through the hollow where the golden-leafed trees stood, angling away from the roo.

She glanced back once. The roo hadn't moved, but as it saw her looking, it raised one heavily-clawed forepaw in something like a wave or a salute—either way it drove a shot of adrenalin through Deena's veins and she nearly slipped in the soft leaf litter.

At the very edge of the gold-leafed trees, where they gave way abruptly to the bright green ones, Deena paused, shivering a little because she hadn't been walking long enough for her body to really heat up, and shockingly enough, the temperature hadn't increased while she'd been with the dragon, and her thick polar fleece jumper had been in her pack, along with her beanie and fingerless gloves.

But the golden trees seemed even more magical than the green-leafed ones, and if she had to somehow magic the trees away, surely this was the place to try. So she paused, and did her best to ignore the kangaroos.

Earlier, it had almost sounded as if the trees were saying her name.

Swallowing heavily, Deena clenched her jaw. She inhaled, then exhaled through puffed out cheeks.

"Um, hi?" she said softly, then cleared her throat and tried again a little louder. "Hello, trees?"

The rustling came as before, something slightly deeper than the wind, more regular, more like the ocean, if each tree were its own beach with its own, rhythmic waves—or if each tree had its own voice, and they were all speaking at once, overlapping.

"Can you… Can you hear me?" Deena ventured.

Deeeeenaaaa, the trees shushed. *Deeeeennnaaaaa.*

They didn't *sound* menacing, just otherworldly, and though their branches waved it was really more of a waft, and just generally around, rather than in her specific direction.

Deena cleared her throat again. "Um, hi," she said. "I, uh, I believe I, um, dreamed you here, is that right?"

Deeenaaa, the trees shushed. *Deeeeennnnaaa.*

She swallowed. "Okay, yeah, that's me. So. If I, uh, brought you here, then, well, I kind of have a favour to ask. I, um. I need you to go away. Please. So I can have my friends back. You know. I'm sorry," she added lamely. "It's nothing personal. I do really like you." It seemed like the polite thing to add, and it certainly wasn't false.

Unfortunately, the trees seemed to disagree.

The wind gusted again, and fistfuls of golden, razor-sharp leaves began raining down on Deena. A couple caught her cheeks and forehead and nose, slicing her skin like fine, deep papercuts.

Deena shouted and covered her face with her hands. "Stop! Stop that!"

But the trees spat more golden blades at her, slicing up her hands.

Deena ran.

Back down the slope she went, skipping steps and jumping boulders, feet pounding in the slippery leaf litter, blood pounding in her ears.

She tripped once, threw out a hand to keep from falling, and the tree's bark burned her where she clutched it.

Tears stung her eyes.

She couldn't say she *blamed* the trees, exactly. If they were trying to get rid of her, she'd probably do the same thing.

But they'd already devoured her friends. Or replaced them, or vanished them; whatever, the point was her friends were gone, and so was the tent, and she had no idea how else to ever see them again if she couldn't get rid of the forest.

Deep breaths, Deena, she told herself. Standing on flat ground over a little knoll just near the base of the mountain, Deena inhaled.

Salt. Sap.

She concentrated on the smells, on the way the green hit the back of her throat, the way the salt air crusted the tears drying on her cheeks, and before too long her pulse began to slow. *There,* she told herself. *Now just stay calm. You've got this.*

What exactly it was that she had, she wasn't quite certain, but whatever it was, she had it, and she wasn't going to let herself panic again.

A kangaroo coughed nearby.

Deena jumped.

To her right, on the flat where the mountain levelled out properly before the ocean, stood the smallest of the kangaroos, staring piercingly at her.

Something shifted in the leaf litter behind, a score or so paces back up the mountain.

The big male kangaroo, thickly muscled and glinty-eyed.

Deena swallowed, rubbing at the goosebumps on her arms. Since when had it gotten so cold?

It was about that moment that her heart lurched, because she realised that although the sky was the same overcast, pearly grey it had been when she'd first struck up the mountain, the quality of the light was different.

Same degree of light, opposite end of the day. Somehow, her climb up the mountain had eaten the daylight.

The kangaroos coughed again, almost in unison, so that one sounded like the echo of the other. They moved closer, and Deena noted that the third kangaroo had joined them, the three of them closing in on her steadily.

Deena chewed the inside of her lip, eyeing them one at a time.

Closer. Closer.

They were coming slowly, but purposefully, like they could get right to her and just keep on going, hopping carefully right through her.

Probably, she decided, it was best to move.

And so she did, and she spent the better part of the next half hour being herded back up the coast by the roos, who as long as she was moving maintained a respectful distance.

The one time she dared halt, abruptly angry about the whole day, like someone had struck a match in her chest, the male kangaroo had come right up to her and bitten her shoulder.

Deena had swatted him on the nose, but he'd only snorted disdainfully at her, and nudged her onward with his head.

And so she'd walked, all the way back from the mountain to the campsite where she'd started the day: a grassy clearing separated by a ridge no taller than Deena from white sand that squeaked down to the ocean. Around it, a stand of the strange, mysterious trees stood straight and tall, their greyish trunks blurring like some magic eye illusion into the distance.

Abruptly, the big male roo flopped down onto his side, reclining on one elbow with his knee up, as though posing for some sort of calendar. He stared at Deena for a moment longer, then put his head down and closed his eyes.

Did… Did kangaroos sleep lying down? Deena didn't think so, although she'd certainly seen them recline before.

Either way, it seemed she'd reached the end of her journey, because the other kangaroos had flopped down similarly on the other side of her, and they mustn't have been expecting her to go anywhere else, because they appeared to be sleeping as well.

Deena glanced up at the heights of the trees here, trunks tall and straight as poles, branches sticking out almost at right angles, coin-sized green leaves shushing like confetti.

She bit her lip. It didn't seem like asking these trees to leave would have any better luck than asking the other ones had.

A kangaroo grunted, and Deena glanced over, but it seemed it had made the noise in its sleep—or doze, or whatever it was doing.

Deena bit her lip some more. Maybe that was it. Maybe… The dragon creature had said she'd dreamed the forest into being, right? Had called it while she slept?

So maybe sleep was the answer. Dream the whole thing away again.

Assuming, of course, that she could figure out how to control her dreams, something she'd never yet managed to achieve, despite the full-colour, hyper-vivid, movie-style visions she was treated to most nights.

Sighing, Deena sat down, legs folded underneath her. That wasn't going to work, of course, so after a short hesitation, she gave up and lay all the way down on her side, knees pulled up to her chest, her underneath arm tucked against the hollow of her neck as a pillow.

The crooks and crevices of the ground pressed against her body; the smell of grasses and wild dirt pressed against her nose; and the taste of the ocean just over the rise filled the back of her throat.

Sleep, she told herself. *Sleep.*

But of course, no matter how she tossed and turned, she couldn't settle, couldn't let herself drift off. As her grandmother used to say of Deena's little cousins, she had no more sleep in her than fly to the moon. And it was cold.

She rolled onto her back for the umpteenth time and sighed heavily.

A kangaroo grunted in response, and Deena glanced over at it. As she watched, it used its long claws to scratch vigorously at one ear, the ear flip-flopping back and forth.

Deena sighed again, letting her head settle straight and staring up at the darkening pearly sky beyond the gently waving tree fronds above her. "You *won't* just go back where you came from, will you?" she murmured. "It would save me a lot of trouble."

The forest didn't seem to hear her.

Probably, Deena thought as she sat up and brushed loose detritus from her shoulders and shook it out of her hair, that was a good thing, because it was unlikely to have responded positively. But still. She buried her face in her hands, momentarily blocking out the smell of dirt with her sweat-tanged hands. Now she had exactly zero idea what to do.

Maybe if she waited until full night she'd be able to sleep better.

Her stomach rumbled and she pressed it with both hands. All her food had been in her pack.

And now that she thought about it, her throat was dry and thirsty, too, and her water had similarly been in her pack.

It was still cold, and her jumper... Yep. It had been in the pack too.

She wasn't going to cry. She was going to get up, walk to the stream, and have a drink, and be sensible and mature about the whole thing.

She was definitely not going to cry.

After a couple of minutes, once she'd convinced her body to agree with her, Deena pressed the liquid from her eyes with firm fingertips and stood up. She stretched, shoulders popping, and brushed herself down.

First things first: water.

Sure, if it got really cold tonight she could die of exposure, and if she survived that long enough the hunger might get her—but water would make both cold and hunger more bearable, and was the most pressing necessity in keeping her alive for the long term.

Even if it was a long term without her friends, stuck in a spontaneous forest with no food and no shelter, and no idea how far the forest stretched.

Would the trees become violent if she started pulling branches to make a shelter? Deena bit her lip as she wove through the trunks, heading for the little stream that flowed out to the sea. Bouncing the inside of her cheek between her teeth, she decided to leave any tree-raiding to the last possible moment of necessity. Yes, it would be cold tonight—the temperature was already starting to drop again, the breeze cutting through her long-sleeved shirt—but she could always dig down into the sand for a bit of extra warmth.

She'd be fine.

She was going to be absolutely, one-hundred-percent fine.

Deena set her shoulders and gritted her teeth as she knelt by the fast-flowing brook, and told herself to stop thinking about the worst. She had other things she should be thinking about, like how to get rid of the forest.

Scooping up cold, fresh-smelling water the colour of very weak tea, Deena sipped, the water freezing her lips and burning her fingers as the breeze shushed over her. She could feel the water down her throat, setting into a knot of cold just below her ribs.

She made herself drink several scoopfuls regardless. Alive was more important than comfortable at this point. "Still," she muttered as she let the dregs of water fall back into the stream. "It wouldn't have killed him to give me a little more assistance. Do you hear that?" she added, louder. "You could have given me more help. You could have told me *how*."

She hadn't meant for her tone to be quite that scathing, but then again, it was a pretty accurate reflection of how she felt. Bloody cryptic dragon, with its bloody servant kangaroos and bland assumption that she'd know just what to do once she got back here.

A kangaroo coughed, right behind her, and Deena jumped like she'd been electrocuted.

"What?" she snapped as the smallest one eyed her warily. "What is it now?"

He did not tell you what to do?

The words bypassed her ears and landed directly in her brain with all the subtlety of using a four-by-two to swat a fly. Deena winced.

We are sorry, the voice came again. *This is why we do not usually talk to mortals. But he did not tell you how to go about dismantling the forest?*

Still wincing, Deena shook her head. "No," she said. "All he told me was that I'd dreamed it into being and had to get rid of it if I wanted to see my friends again."

He is angry with us still, another voice chimed in, and, hands clapped over her ears even though it didn't help, Deena turned to see the huge male kangaroo only an arm's length away.

He shouldn't be, the third kangaroo chimed in. *It has been many, many years since he was punished.*

The smallest kangaroo shrugged. *You know how he holds onto these things. If a grudge is to be kept, it is to be kept by him.*

Hands still pressing over her ears—for the psychological comfort if nothing else—Deena turned to the roos, wide-eyed. "You mean... You're not his servants?"

The male kangaroo spat abruptly, and the other two gave a coughing kind of grunt. Deena shrank away.

No, the male said, loud enough to make bells ring in Deena's head. *We are no servants of that trickster.*

"Trick... Trickster?" Deena's heart pounded. *Oh no. Oh no oh no oh no.*

The smallest roo laid a sharp-clawed paw on Deena's shoulder. *There, there, little one. What he told you was true enough, that you did dream this forest into being. But for the sake of his grudge with us, he was not fair to you. He did not tell you the whole truth.*

"Why... Why would that matter to you?" The whole thing was really no more surreal than anything else that had happened today, but the thought of being caught in a decades-long grudge between a mob of kangaroos and a plant dragon who lived in another plane of existence was really too much. Deena giggled, because it was that or break down sobbing.

The third kangaroo gave her a stern look.

Because he knows that, once again, we will have to fix his mess, the smallest kangaroo said scathingly.

You may have called the forest, the male added, *but to call it on such a scale as this?* He swept the forest around them with a wide gesture of his forepaw. *That is not within the powers of a human.*

He tricked you, the third kangaroo said. *He used you for his purposes. He knows that we cannot survive in a forest such as this, for it was born from magic, and will drain our magic to survive.*

He means to kill us, the small one said, *and be released from his prison once and for all.*

Deena was quite sure that her eyes would fall out of her head in a moment. "What… What can I do?"

The kangaroos shrugged. *You must unmake it,* the third kangaroo said, twitching its ears back and forth.

"But I can't," Deena said. "I've tried."

Oh, yes, the small one said, scathing yet again. *You asked so politely, did you not.*

Abruptly, Deena bristled, indignation rising from her stomach like heat. "Well I don't know what else to do," she said. "And no one's been exactly *forthcoming* with information on what else I should try, have they."

Go swimming, the third kangaroo said. *Your life will be in danger, so do not swim too far.*

Deena's eyebrows skyrocketed at almost launch velocity. "If it will put my life in danger, why on earth would I do it?"

Because if you do not, your friends will die. And so will we.

You must control your gift, the huge male added. *You must reset the balance of the world here to free them.*

"But I told you," Deena snapped, hands fisting at her sides. "I *tried.* I don't know what to *do.* You say the dragon didn't tell me everything, and I bloody well *know* that. He barely told me anything! But you lot are hardly any better, with your vague 'go swimming, don't die' pieces of advice!"

The forest is huge, its magic vast. To unmake it, it is vital that you control your gift with a finesse beyond your years. But to control your gift at all, you must confront it. And for one so ignorant as yourself, the only way to confront it is to scare it out of hiding by threatening your own life.

Deena opened her mouth, preparing for some sort of cutting remark—but the creature's comment did have a strange kind of logic behind it. "Okay," she said cautiously instead. "And if I do this, if I... go swimming, this will get my friends back?"

Only if you are successful.

"And if I'm not?" She was proud; her voice barely tremored at all.

You die. They die. We all die.

Ring-a-ring-a-rosies, Deena didn't have time to add before the small one continued, *And this forest here will grow to take over the world.* She waved her claws in a gesture that was only just short of menacing.

You poured too much into it, the male rejoined, chiding.

Deena puffed up, indignant. "Well it wasn't exactly like I knew what I was doing!"

The kangaroos gave her a long, level look. *All the more reason for you to have been careful in the first place.*

Deena's hands found her hips. Her skin was goose bumping, her lips probably turning blue, but she ignored that for the moment. "You said it was the dragon that made the forest this big, anyway! It isn't even my fault!"

All three of them merely stared at her.

Deena held their gaze as long as she could, but... *if* they were telling the truth (a big 'if' at this point), then there really was nothing else for it. Her fault or not, the dragon certainly wasn't going to do anything more to save them, so she had to try. With the best flounce she could muster in dirty, sweaty hiking gear in the middle of a magic forest as the light died away and the temperatures began to plummet, Deena turned and began stripping off her boots.

What are you doing?

That was the female, and the alarm in her voice gave Deena pause; she glanced back over her shoulder at the smallest roo. "Going swimming."

Not here, the roo replied, and Deena could sense, if not see, the eyes rolling. *In the ocean! This water does not contain sufficient power.*

Deena stared blankly at the kangaroos, gaze moving from one silvered face to the next.

Abruptly, she whirled away, one brown hiking boot still in her hand, wafting sweaty foot smell and she stomped toward the beach, muttering. "Go swimming, they say. In the bloody ocean, they say. Not like it's dropping below double digits and I have no way to make a fire or anything. Don't swim too deep!" she mimicked. "It might kill you! Yeah, well, I know exactly why it might kill me, and that's because it's too bloody *cold* to go swimming in the ocean. This is madness. Sparta," she added as she reached the sand and kicked the other boot off emphatically. "That's what this is. Sparta."

With tight, jerky movements, Deena stripped out of her hiking socks, her pants, her long-sleeved wicking shirt. She grabbed her merino-wool singlet at the hem, arms crossed, bracing to pull out of it… but no. Some insulation in the water might be helpful, and wool was a good insulator even if it was wet. With a tug, she straighten the hem of the teal-blue singlet and raised her chin.

"Fine," she snapped at no one in particular. "I am going swimming."

She marched to the wet sand line—and shuddered as the sun slipped below the hills behind her and the chill of night's shadows overtook her. "Deena," she told herself, "you had better bloody well be dreaming."

She took a couple of steps forward, the salt wind twining around her. She wrapped her arms around her ribcage and tried to pretend like her teeth weren't chattering as her toes hit the water, icy and unforgiving.

The light was draining from the sky awfully fast, and in front of Deena the ocean stretched dark and restless. Even the sand seemed grey, and Deena bit her lip hard.

This wasn't going to get any easier.

Deena yelled, a cry that she hoped was blood-curdling but which was, at the very least, a little motivating, and she ran into the surf. For the first few strides she lifted her knees high, and the yell turned to more of a scream as freezing spray hit her midriff.

Then her feet caught in the cold, swishing sand, and she tripped, and fell.

At least the shriek that escaped her lungs kept her from inhaling the salty water as she fell under it.

She surfaced, shivering, pressing water from her eyes—and immediately crouched back down again. Now that she was in, the sea water was much warmer than the wind-chilled air.

So Deena crouched, fanning her hands like a shrimp to keep herself mostly steady as gentle waves rocked in and out, in and out, the smell of salt around her, the taste of it on her lips, wondering what on earth she was supposed to do now.

Threaten her life.

She snorted.

Well, if nothing else, she could just sit here for another ten minutes or so; much longer than that in water like this and she'd be threatening her life with hypothermia. She could already feel her lips turning blue.

Deena pressed her fingers against her mouth, but it didn't help; it only emphasised how the breeze cut against her cheek bones, the tip of her nose—and the tips of her fingers.

Bloody fracking *cold*, that's what it was, although leaving the singlet on had been a solid choice; the wool definitely did its job as it tugged and swayed in little movements over her skin.

But the other problem, of course, other than the cold, was that there wasn't a plant to be seen—nearby, anyway, since there were obviously plenty on the shore. How was she supposed to awaken this apparent talent of hers without any plants nearby?

Maybe if she moved more she'd be warmer.

Quickly, Deena breaststroked out a little further, until she could just about stand submerged to her neck between the waves, bobbing up like a cork as each one passed. It was a soothing kind of motion, like lazy, dreamy jumping, and combined with the cold it lulled her mind.

Once, she snorted and gurgled as water went up her nose—she'd been drifting, she realised, falling asleep right here in the waves.

Maybe the danger wasn't something large and frightful after all, but simply this: the slow, inevitable drift toward sleep, body and mind numbed by the cold, by the motion.

Something caressed her foot.

Deena squeaked and jerked away faster than she'd have thought possible with her body this cold.

The thing brushed against her again.

It was almost entirely dark now, just the slightest glimmer of teal twilight curving against the horizon—and so it took all the courage she had left to reach her arm down in the water, to stretch toward the *thing* that seemed to stretch back.

Her fingers brushed the thing, soft, slimy... Seaweed, she realised.

Her heart unclenched and the adrenalin drained away, her pulse falling back into a sleepy kind of background beat. Just seaweed. It twined about her fingers, silky soft and strong, tugging, caressing, kissing her skin.

Deena's eyes were closed again, and she didn't remember closing them. But the seaweed, the kelp, whatever it specifically was, was soft, and gentle, and calming.

I could rest, she thought, and she wasn't sure if the thought had come from within or without. *Just keep my eyes closed here for a while, regain my strength...* Strength like the gentle, inexorable rocking of the ocean, or the grip of the thick weed twining and banding about her ankles, her calves, her legs, drawing her down slowly, so slowly, into its embrace.

The plant, Deena realised abruptly, loved her, and she smiled underwater as it hugged her, growing and stretching and lengthening just for her, because she loved it, and it loved her so, so much in return.

She was underwater.

She was underwater, and she wasn't cold any more.

Adrenalin punched through her awareness.

Fire lit in her lungs.

Deena wondered how long it had been since she'd last taken a breath—and as she did, panic welled.

She fought it down, thrashing a little as the seaweed tightened its embrace.

Her heart hammered.

Air. She needed air.

But the plant had her trapped.

In just a few more seconds, she was going to run out of oxygen, and she was going to die.

Deena opened her eyes under the water, but it was dark, and it didn't help.

Pressure built in her sinuses, across her face, as her body screamed for air. With her free hand, she pinched her nose closed tight, and she pursed her lips hard to block the impulse to scream, to open her mouth—to breathe.

Then, she remembered what the kangaroos had said.

Threaten your life so that your talent will be forced into the open—or words to that effect, her vision was starting to get spotty despite the darkness and it was hard to remember exactly.

Her talent. Her gift, her whatever it was—this sense that the plant around her adored her and was prepared to kill her for that.

Or, well, not *prepared*, it probably didn't realise that it was going to extinguish the source of its adoration by piling the love on too thick, but Deena knew the *gist* of what she meant: this plant loved her, and because of that it was growing so fast and strong that it would kill her if she couldn't convince it to back off.

So, *No,* she told it firmly as her lungs burned for air. *No, this is not like the trees. You may be long, and strong, and capable of pulling me down, but I will. not. let you. I love you too,* she said. *But you have to let me go.*

Deena felt something golden leave her, a burst of light or warmth or something—and the kelp shrank back.

Something inside Deena's mind went 'click'.

For a long, tortuous heartbeat, the pain of oxygen deprivation vanished and Deena could see it, suddenly, like a complex maths problem that suddenly made sense, a formula made clear, an ambiguous sentence that abruptly came into focus: there, that was the way to manipulate the plants, to make them grow—or shrink. To bend them to her desires.

She stretched out her hand beneath the waves, wrapped by coldness and dark, and felt the power trickle outward.

Away, she murmured, quiet even in the privacy of her own mind. *Back to sleep now. Away.*

Sure enough, the kelp began to furl back in on itself, a slow, lazy motion like sleep. The fronds drifted away from her arms, her legs, and gradually disappeared into the darkness with something akin to a peaceful, contented sigh.

She'd done it. She was free.

Deena was free, but she was too cold, too tired, too *spent* to move.

The fire in her lungs came rushing back.

It would be easy—so, so easy—to just take a breath, draw the water in, give up and go to sleep as well.

This was it, then. She'd mastered the power, but she was going to die anyway, with her lungs on fire and sleep in her bones.

Claws wrapped around her wrist, puncturing the soft skin—just another fierce pain along with the pain in her lungs, the intense burn of cold at her fingers, her feet, her face. She struggled toward the claws, gasping and coughing as her head broke the surface—and in the clear light of the risen moon, Deena saw the profile of the big male kangaroo, his buff chest rippling as he helped haul her free, up, up, out.

Deena struggled, kicking at the sand, stroking weakly with her free arm as they stretched for the shore—only to drop, coughing, onto the wet sand at the tideline, the ocean kissing at her legs as though to apologise for its role in what had been done.

The air was frigid. Goosebumps covered Deena in an instant, and she knew if she didn't get back into her clothes—soon—she was as good as dead anyway.

But the clothes were several paces away, up the beach on the dry sand, and here where the water lapped over her, she could pretend that the water was warm.

It was, in comparison to the air, anyway.

And, she noted blearily, the trees were still there, casting their dark silhouettes against the star-spangled sky.

If she'd had any energy left at all, she'd have used it to cry.

Something warm pressed against her back. The kangaroo, leaning up against her, its fur wet and slicked down from its dip in the ocean, but a warm body nonetheless.

She rolled over and wrapped herself around it, shivering and shaking as she buried her fingers in its thick fur.

There was a little grunt behind her, and suddenly another warm weight at her back, this one dry—and then something was tugging at her legs, twisting her up and away from the waves, and she managed to get mostly up on all fours and half crawl, half let herself be pushed toward the dry sand, and her clothing.

Her teeth were chattering.

The sand felt frosty under her palms, her knees. She coughed, and salt water burned the back of her throat.

She spat it out, wiped her mouth with the back of one hand—and when she put her hand back down again, cool fabric met her fingers.

Wet things off first, came the voice of the smallest kangaroo, still ringing Deena's head like a gong, but manageable now she was used to it.

Shuddering, Deena fumbled at the hem of her woollen singlet. It took a few goes with numb fingers, but slowly, she inched it off—and then her bra, and her undies.

The kangaroos pressed against her from all directions, fur cool in the night air but body heat warm underneath, and as Deena skinned into her hiking shirt, her leggings, and her pants, the biting cold subsided just a little. She still shuddered violently every few moments, her teeth were still chattering, but she was clothed, and she was alive.

The big male roo backed off a few steps and shook vigorously before rolling in the sand. There was something vaguely comical about his huge hind legs splayed toward the sky.

Deena clutched at the smallest kangaroo, who obligingly planted herself in Deena's lap as the third roo pressed up against her back, and after some indefinite period of time, Deena realised she could feel her fingers properly again—though not her toes, because her legs were going to sleep with the weight of the kangaroo on them.

She inhaled deeply. The beach smelled different at night, still salty, but the mineral smell of the sand seemed more noticeable in the dark and the cold.

The trees, said the third kangaroo. *Time is running out.*

The moon, Deena realised, was more than halfway across the sky. "What happens if I haven't done it by dawn?" She made it through the whole sentence without her teeth chattering, and for the first time, dared to let herself hope that maybe she would survive the night.

The forest wins, the small kangaroo said simply. *And we will fade.*

Adrenalin squeezed Deena's heart briefly. Rachel. The boys. And what would she tell their parents?

Deena pressed her face down against the small kangaroo's back, nostrils thick with the smell of musty fur, something like a dog but wilder, more subtle, less tamed.

It had to be done.

And so, with her fingers curled in the kangaroo's fur and her legs prickling with pins and needles, the sand cold underneath her and the air chilling her face, Deena leaned against the warmth of the kangaroo behind her, closed her eyes, and opened that strange sense she'd discovered while she'd been underwater.

With her eyes closed, she could feel the plants around her, as though each one emitted a gentle hum on a slightly different frequency. The tall, straight trees with their rough grey-brown bark and coin-round emerald-green leaves were something like a middle C, she decided, their hum like the noise of a live power line.

The grasses were higher pitched, a small cacophony of sharp sounds like crickets, trilling boldly in the night.

The saltbushes were a crackling, shushing kind of hum, and far away beneath it all, Deena thought she could just detect a gentle, haunting sound as of otherworldly pipes: the kelp forests out off shore.

It was the trees she focused on now, sending out a wave of gentle sleepiness as she had to the kelp in the ocean.

Sleep, she told the trees. *Go away now and sleep, until I need you again. Sleep.*

Deena yawned hard, her jaw cracking, her mouth filling with the taste of salty air.

Sleep, trees. Go to sleep.

She leaned back against the kangaroo, her head lolling to one side as the wave of sleep overtook her, sweeping her along with the gentle humming sound of the trees.

Sleep.

Deena rolled onto one side, sandwiched between two warm bodies, cradled by the sand. She shifted, bending her lower arm to cushion her head, pausing to scoop out the sand a little more to make a hollow for her shoulder.

Sleep, my lovely trees. Sleep. I'll see you again.

Now her upper hip was cold, and after a little while longer the lower one began to hurt as it poked into the ground.

Deena shifted again, inhaling a sigh that smelled of cold night air and slightly-musty down. She drew something soft under her head and plumped it sleepily under her neck.

Sleep.

She'd only just drifted off when a zipper zzzz'ed in the quiet of the night.

Blasted Rachel, always sneaking off the boys' tent and waking Deena up at the most inconvenient moments. "Shhhh," Deena whispered, pulling her sleeping bag back up over her cold hip as something gave a marsupial cough in the night. "Be quiet," she thought she added, though she couldn't be sure.

They were supposed to be being quiet, it was important; something was going to sleep now.

Deena dreamed more than saw Rachel mouthing 'Sorry' as she slipped into her own sleeping bag, a dark, misshapen lump on the other side of the tent. Deena sniffed and went back to sleep, and the night was quiet for a time, disturbed only by the chirping of the crickets, the quiet, high-pitched noises of the grass, and a low, deep shushing from the gum trees all around.

Deena froze, curled on one side, heart suddenly pumping with adrenalin.

Her neck was on a pillow, or at least the wad of jumpers she shoved into a thin bag to make a pillow.

Her body was warm, cosy... like she was in a sleeping bag.

And if she held her breath, carefully, like so... was that more breathing she could hear, right behind her?

Probably, it was the kangaroos.

But awareness was filtering in now, and through closed eyelids she could sense light, and as she cracked her lids open, she saw sunlight dappling the pale inside of the tent.

Heart pounding, breaths shallow, Deena rolled slowly over, savouring the musty scent of the air in the tent, caused by old sleeping bags and largely unwashed humans.

Rachel lay on the opposite side of the tent, mouth slightly open, brown hair plastered over half her face as she curled around her own makeshift pillow.

Deena's chest buoyed, and she bit her lip.

Only…

She frowned.

Deena was known for her hyper-realistic dreams. Her friends often told her that she cried out while she slept, or else sat up and uttered some strange prognostication before lying back down and resuming her sleep.

It was too wild, too implausible, to think it had been anything more than just that.

She sighed, and resigned herself to putting a strange, awfully realistic dream out of her head just as the boys called 'knock knock' at the door of the tent and crouched to let themselves in.

Rachel squeaked sleepily, pulling the bottle-green sleeping bag up to her chin so she looked like some kind of pale-faced caterpillar. "I'm not dressed," she mumbled.

"Hold on," Deena told the boys. "We're coming."

She slithered out of her own bag as Rachel sat up and rummaged in her pack for clothing.

Deena knelt—and paused. She was still in her hiking pants, and the shirt she'd worn yesterday.

Surely… She never slept in her hiking pants. They were filthy, and uncomfortable, and her leggings were far, far preferable as pyjamas.

She stood, and as she did it was her turn to squeak, because something had stabbed her thigh.

"What?" Rachel asked. "What is it?"

Deena shoved her hand into her pocket, and withdrew a twig—greyish brown, with leaves the size of coins—and the colour of bright, metallic gold, half crushed and folded from their stint in her pocket.

The zip of the tent zzzzed and the boys' faces appeared, concern making little vertical lines at the inner corners of their brows. "What's wrong? Are you okay?"

Rachel squeaked some more, as though she hadn't just spent the night in their tent with them. Deena would have rolled her eyes, but she was too busy starting at the golden leaves, glimmering and glowing in the soft morning light of the tent.

"Whoa," one of the boys breathed, eyes going round. "Where did you find that?"

Deena didn't answer, but passed the twig to his outstretched fingers.

He turned the twig over and over and over, examining the leaves minutely, folding one gently in the very tips of his fingers. When he looked back up at Deena, his face was simultaneously glowing with excitement, his eyes alight, and coloured by confusion, brows tilted, mouth a little tight. "Deena," he said. "These look like real gold. What the hell?"

Deena took them back, grinning fiercely. She twirled the twig in front of her, feeling everyone's eyes on her. "You wouldn't believe me if I told you," she said. "You'd tell me I was dreaming."

Abruptly, Rachel, who had clearly been dressing

in her sleeping bag all this time, leapt out and caught Deena in a tight, squishy hug. "That's 'cause you're always dreaming," she said.

Deena laughed, and the boys piled into the tent as well, one of them shouting, "Group hug!"

They squished around her, strong arms holding her tight while Deena waved the twig of golden leaves in the air so they didn't get ruined, and laughed while tears spilled over her cheeks.

Her friends were back.

Through the slit in the tent's flaps, she could make out the forest around them—and it was bushland again, tea tree and wattles and gum trees, just like it should always have been.

Only this time, when she pressed her eyes closed and her face into Rachel's shoulder, while the boys wrapped their strong, warm arms around them, through the smell of sweat-soaked clothing and dirty hiking gear, Deena could still sense the lingering trace of sap in the air, and if she listened very, very carefully, she could hear it: the sound of the trees themselves, growing hard in the morning light. She could feel it, too, for the trees and the other plants loved her—and Deena loved them back.

She didn't care if everyone thought she was dreaming, because now she knew for certain: those days in her grandmother's garden had been no accident, no flight of childhood fancy. Magic was here, magic was real—and it was hers.

ABOUT THE AUTHOR

AMY LAURENS is an Australian author of fantasy and science fiction for both adults and young adults. She also writes non-fiction books, often on various aspects of writing. Also dogs. Lots of dogs.

After completing a university education involving many twists and turns, through more faculties than ought reasonably to exist, Amy now spends her day as a high-school English teacher. No, she is not going to do your homework for you. Not even the English bit. Sorry. Have a cookie instead.

Amy has published 14 titles to date. Her most recent release is *How Not To Acquire A Castle*, a humorous fantasy novel for readers of all ages that follows Mercury's attempts to graduate at the top of the Evil Overlord class and acquire herself a castle. If you like Terry Pratchett's *Discworld*, you'll appreciate Mercury.

FREE EBOOK

Thank you for buying this book!

When you buy an Inkprint Press book in print, we like to thank you by offering you the ebook for free. Please head to:

http://www.inkprintpress.com/amy-laurens/dreaming-of-forests/

And use the coupon DOFPRINT to download your free copy in both .mobi and .epub formats. (The coupon will only work once.)

Read more by Amy Laurens!

WHERE SHADOWS RISE

CHAPTER ONE

THE DOORBELL RANG. That doesn't sound exciting in and of itself, but let me assure you: it was the most heart-pounding thing to happen all week. It was my birthday, I was home alone, and because of the stupid witness protection business, I'd been stuck in the house all summer. I hadn't even been allowed out to see friends, because we'd arrived in town at the end of last year with only three school weeks to go—so I didn't have any friends.

Well. I had friends, but they were back in Melbourne, and I wasn't allowed to contact them for fear someone would track down our new location. Lucky me.

Anyway, it was my birthday, I was alone because Mum and Dad had gone to do something regarding birthday surprises and Anna had inexplicably chosen to go with them, and the door-bell had just rung. I stared at the closed door, heart pounding, while our chocolate Labrador, Veve, tried to chew it down. Was I going to open it?

Of course I was going to open it. The chances of it being a mobster were slim to none; for starters, a mobster wouldn't have rung the bell.

I opened it.

"Miss Tanning?" The deliveryman raised a questioning eyebrow and cocked a digital pen at me.

I nodded, heart flip-flopping, and scrawled a fair impersonation of my signature on the digital pad.

He handed over a small, brown-paper parcel with a handwritten address, and departed.

I closed the door behind him, throat dry, and stared down at Veve. On the one hand, yay birthday present. On the other, holy crap, someone had our address. That was *not* a good thing.

It became even less of a good thing when I noticed that the parcel was indeed addressed to a Miss Tanning: a Miss *Anna* Tanning, as in my sister, not me, Emma Tanning.

Anger bubbled up in my chest, hot and tight, and the parcel protested in my grip.

Veve whined softly.

"How could she *do* this?" I whispered to Veve.

I turned the parcel over. It was from Kade, Anna's frogging ex-boyfriend. Who apparently wasn't an 'ex' after all.

Urgh. I ground my teeth. "You know what?" I asked Veve.

She looked up at me with her liquid brown eyes, tongue lolling as she smiled.

"Screw it. If Anna can get interstate mail from people who aren't even supposed to know we exist anymore, you and I can go for a walk on my birthday. What do you think?"

They say dogs don't speak English, but Veve sure as heck knew the word 'walk'—though I think in her vocabulary it was something closer to 'Magical Trip To Disneyland' and less like 'Comparatively Bland Meander Through Trees'.

She tucked her tail right under her butt and shot down the hall, whirling in frantic circles a few times at the end before pelting back as I retrieved her lead from the drawer in the front cabinet.

I rolled my eyes as I clipped her lead onto her collar. For my troubles, I got slimed right up the nostrils. "You're disgusting, you know that?" I wiped off the worst of the dog slobber on the shoulder of my shirt. She just grinned.

Out on the street, she leapt and twisted madly. "Hair-brain," I told her, snapping the lead to get her attention. "It's just a walk."

She just snorted—and stiffened.

I followed her gaze to where a flock of corellas pecked their way through the dry grass at the end of the street.

"Veve!"

My shout was in vain: the lead burned through my fingers and Veve shot down the road, a chocolate bullet howling death and destruction for all things feathered.

I cursed her to the lower circles of doggie hell. Which probably involved, I don't know, a world devoid of birds, cats, people, sunshine, and walks, if Veve was anything to go by.

"Veve!" If the sight of the mad Lab-rat barrelling toward them hadn't scared the birds off, my shouts would have. "Come back here *now*!"

Predictably, she ignored me, pounding down the slope, through the fringe of gum trees, and down the narrow stairs between giant granite boulders that led to the river.

"Stupid frogging brainless beast of a stupid frogging dog," I muttered as I followed. "If Mum gets home before we do and freaks out, I swear, I'll pluck your tail hairs out."

Empty threats, obviously, but Mum's freak-out wouldn't be. Her thoughts would go straight to the day Anna nearly died—and I wouldn't blame her.

I should have left a note. Urgh.

The stairs ended and I found myself on a track broad enough for two twisting along a creek the colour of bitter tea. Tussock grass clustered in spikes—where the eucalypts would let it—and hot summer sunlight glinted from the leaves. Somewhere to my right, downstream and in the opposite direction to the house, Veve barked. I exhaled like a whale coming up for air and set out after her.

Veve bounded out from the undergrowth in front of me, a dolphin leaping through water, tongue flapping with every bound. "Stupid mutt," I told her under my breath.

She didn't care what I thought (of course), and saved a leap for the last minute so she could plant muddy feet on my hips as I tried to catch her collar.

I straightened, about to insult her some more, and realised that she'd gone stiff again, ears pricked and mouth tight, listening down the path.

My neck prickled. Someone was coming. A second later, I heard footsteps in the gravel, and a low, male voice, humming, or maybe singing softly.

My chest constricted, and just as suddenly my hands were slick. Chances were it was just a stranger out for a midday stroll, but my stomach wound knots about my memories and I smelled the hot concrete and melting asphalt, old oil and stale urine of the Lilydale train station where the body had been hidden in a toilet stall, the body of the girl who'd looked like Anna.

I had to get off the path.

"Come on, Veve," I said, pulling her close, white-knuckled as I stepped into the undergrowth. The tea tree scrub protested, but I shoved my way through anyway, glancing over my shoulder as the humming grew louder.

I kept going until I couldn't hear footsteps any more, until the wind swallowed the hum that sounded too like the warning cry of a hive—danger, we're working here, come close and get stung. I didn't want to get stung; visions of a blood-streaked face refused to be blinked away.

Only Veve tugging brought me back to myself, and I realised firstly that I was holding the lead way too tight, cutting off Veve's air supply, secondly that the reason my cheeks were suddenly cold was because I'd been crying, and thirdly that I'd found the creek again, looping back parallel maybe fifty meters or so from the path.

Abruptly, I dropped Veve's lead and strode forward to kneel by the water. I dipped my hands in. A shiver slid through me at its chill, and I scooped it up to wash my face.

Flinging the excess water away, I gulped at the air, deep, calming breaths all the way down into my belly, and visualised a river washing away the blood from my thoughts, just like the police psych had taught me.

Once the space behind my eyes was calm and black, I drew in one last forceful breath, and opened my eyes. Perched on a rock by the creek, I hugged my knees to my chest as cool water lapped at my toes. Veve was a little upstream, just before the creek bent back toward the path, doggy paddling in circles in a deep spot where the water broadened to maybe ten meters across. In front of me it was broad but shallow, only ankle deep, its path torn to white foam by the rocks.

And—I gasped. In the middle of the stream, glittering in the sun like a piece of fallen sky, was the hugest butterfly I'd ever seen.

Which was pretty huge; besides the fact that I grew up visiting the Melbourne Zoo with its impressive butterfly house every Christmas since I could remember, Mum and Dad had taken us up to Brisbane for a family holiday two years ago, and we'd seen giant tropical butterflies bigger than my hand.

This one, bright blue with black edging like a Ulysses, was bigger than both my hands put together.

And then it turned around.

Okay. I'd grown up reading fairy tales as much as the next person, and although I'd had a horse-crazy stage instead of a fairy-crazy stage like Anna had, I'd seen all her paraphernalia.

Still, none of it prepared me for finding something that looked exactly like a fairy, standing smack in the middle of a creek in boring, back-water Nowra.

I'm pretty sure my eyes were only hanging in their sockets by a thread.

And then it talked.

Her face lit up like a cloud had just uncovered the sun as she spotted me. "Hi there!" she said, fluttering over.

I just stared, heart pounding against my ribcage as though it wanted to run away from the absurdity of it all. "No," I said. "I'm hallucinating."

The fairy frowned. "I don't think so."

I shook my head. "No. No, things like this do not happen. Things like this aren't *real*." I stood, backing up a step.

The fairy sighed. "I promise. I'm quite real."

"You would say that, wouldn't you," I said, eyeing her. "Veve!" I waved at the dog and hopped from one foot to the other, trying to lure her in with the promise of play. "We're going now!"

Veve, adorable beast that she was, landed a little upstream and shook vigorously before trotting toward me. I backed hurriedly away from the bank, dancing to keep Veve's attention.

"Wait!" the fairy cried, wings snapping out and propelling her a couple of feet into the air. "You're a Traveller! I need to talk to you!"

"Uh huh, sure," I said as I wound the lead around

my hand and set off back into the bushes. This was punishment for leaving the house, obviously. The universe was out to get me, reminding me forcefully that once you started disregarding some rules, who knew what other rules you'd end up flouting.

The rules of physics, for example.

I glanced back once, right before the bushes hid the stream altogether. Blue flashed, high up, but I ducked to get a better view and it was only the sky. I scowled. Stupid fairy. Stupid universe. Served me right for leaving the house in the first place. Urgh. "Come on, Veve," I said, snapping the lead. "Even if the house is prison, at least it's *sane*."

I was stomping so furiously as I burst out onto the path that when a figure rose from a stoop only a couple of steps away, I squeaked in surprise.

I scowled. People rarely surprised me; usually I could tell without trying that someone was near. I really must have been off in my own little world.

I glowered at the boy who lived to make my school life a misery. "What are you doing here?" I snapped. "Isn't it bad enough that I have to deal with you on school days? Which, by the way, don't start until tomorrow. You're ruining my holidays."

Okay, so maybe that was a little harsh, but come on. It was *Scott*. I'd arrived in town with three weeks left in the school year, and he'd spent every day of them humiliating me in front of his mates, and I didn't care for a repeat this year.

Scott eyed me warily, which was a strange expression on him.

Usually he strode around like he knew without a doubt that he was too good for the world, and also—somewhere deeper, somewhere I'd only caught a glimpse of once or twice—that it had nothing left to throw at him that could hurt.

Occasionally, in my more generous moments, I wondered what had happened to make him look that way. Mostly, however, I just wondered why he was such a moron.

"What are you doing here?" he asked, voice dripping with accusation and suspicion.

My hands fisted of their own accord, and beside me Veve's hackles rose as she chimed in with a low-pitched, rumbling growl. I flicked the free end of the lead at her nose. "Nothing," I said, in a rousing blaze of wit. "What are you doing?"

He scowled. "You shouldn't be here."

For one heart-stopping instant I thought he meant out here generally, walking around, as if he knew what had happened and why I'd hidden away all summer. Then I realised he was nodding into the undergrowth. I rolled my eyes. "I might be a city slicker," I bit off, "but I'm not stupid. I made enough noise to scare off a herd of elephants, let alone any snakes that might have been lying around." The thought chilled me, though; I *hadn't* been thinking about snakes when I'd hurried off the path. One badly-timed footstep and a brown snake bite later, and I could be a dead body too.

But Scott had moved on, stalking off down the path. He had nice shoulders, I'd give him that much. Pity he couldn't derive his personality from them, instead of whatever dead weight it was he kept inside his head for brains.

Beside me, Veve growled again, louder this time, more urgent. I snapped the lead at her and stared after Scott's retreating form, trying to think of something cutting.

It was only when Veve growled for the third time that I realised she wasn't even facing Scott. Instead, she was looking back into the bushes—and something dark was flickering in there, deep in the shadows of the trees.

My chest squeezed in on itself and adrenalin shot through my body. Veve's growling grew louder until it broke in a bark, something midway between slavering and terrified, and I realised my tongue was stuck to the roof of my mouth. Carefully I peeled it away, unable to tear my eyes from the shifting darkness in the bushes. There was no discernible form, just shadow, darker than it should have been this soon after midday, and a pervasive sense of dread clamping down on me like an on-coming storm.

Veve began backing away, hackles prickling, growl rising and falling like thunder. I glanced down at her, back to the shadows—and they were closer, much closer than they had been.

I turned and bolted.

Keep reading! Head to
http://www.amylaurens.com/books/sanctuary/where-shadows-rise/
to buy your copy now!